For Dad and all those guardians
who watch over us in unexpected ways.

ABOUT THIS BOOK

The art for this book was created using paper cutouts, crayons, acrylic paint,
and digital collage. This book was edited by Andrea Spooner and designed by Patrick Collins
with art direction from Saho Fujii. The production was supervised by Patricia Alvarado,
and the production editor was Jake Regier. The text was set in Neutra Text Book Alt,
and the display type is hand lettered.

Copyright © 2022 by Marcelo Verdad • Cover illustration copyright © 2022 by Marcelo Verdad •
Cover design by Saho Fujii and Patrick Collins • Cover copyright © 2022 by Hachette Book Group, Inc. • Hachette Book Group
supports the right to free expression and the value of copyright. The purpose of copyright is to encourage writers and artists to produce
the creative works that enrich our culture. • The scanning, uploading, and distribution of this book without permission is a theft of the
author's intellectual property. If you would like permission to use material from the book (other than for review purposes), please contact
permissions@hbgusa.com. Thank you for your support of the author's rights. • Little, Brown and Company • Hachette Book Group •
1290 Avenue of the Americas, New York, NY 10104 • Visit us at LBYR.com • First Edition: October 2022 • Little, Brown and Company is a
division of Hachette Book Group, Inc. • The Little, Brown name and logo are trademarks of Hachette Book Group, Inc. • The publisher is
not responsible for websites (or their content) that are not owned by the publisher. • Library of Congress Cataloging-in-Publication Data •
Names: Verdad, Marcelo, author, illustrator. • Verdad, Marcelo, illustrator. • Title: The worst teddy ever / Marcelo Verdad. • Description:
First edition. • New York : Little, Brown and Company, 2022. • Audience: Ages 4–8. • Summary: "Noa is frustrated that Teddy is
always too tired to play with him, but little does he know that Teddy is awake all night keeping him safe from night visitors." —Provided by
publisher. • Identifiers: LCCN 2021033041 • ISBN 9780316330459 (hardcover) • Subjects: CYAC: Teddy bears—Fiction. • Classification:
LCC PZ7.1.V455 Wo 2022 • DDC [E]—dc23 • LC record available at https://lccn.loc.gov/2021033041 • ISBN 978-0-316-33045-9 •
Printed in the United States of America • PHX • 10 9 8 7 6 5 4 3 2 1

The Worst Teddy EVER

marcelo verdad

LB
LITTLE, BROWN AND COMPANY
New York   Boston

Noa LOVES Teddy.

They do everything together.

Or at least they TRY to.

But Teddy...

Teddy is ALWAYS tired!

Other kids have AWESOME cuddly friends that love them and play with them all day long.

But Teddy...

Teddy is always too sleepy
to do what Noa wants.

Sometimes, Noa thinks that
Teddy is the worst teddy EVER!

During the night, a little ghost
stops by.

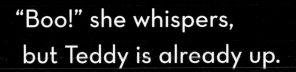

"Boo!" she whispers,
but Teddy is already up.

"I know you're scared of the dark, little ghost," Teddy says, and he offers a flashlight.

"But no visitors are allowed at night. You'll have to say goodbye."

Just as Teddy makes sure that
Noa is still fast asleep…

...the Boogeyman breaks in!

"I'm BORED!" the Boogeyman growls,
so Teddy gives him some toys.

"I know you just want to play, but no
visitors are allowed at night. You'll
have to say goodbye."

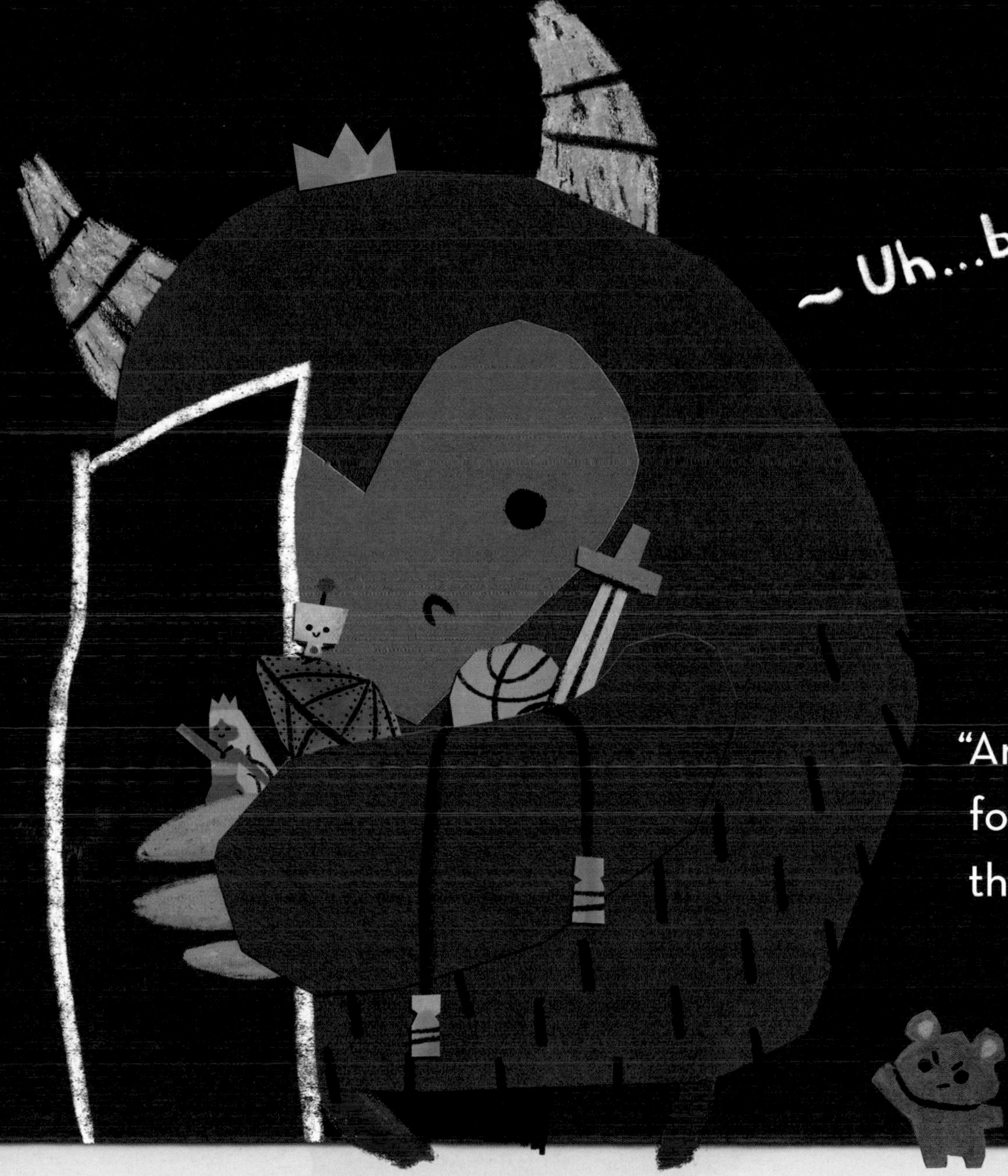

"And don't forget to bring them back!"

Teddy keeps an eye on Noa until...

...the Tooth Fairy
pops in!

TOYS

"I've come to collect some teeth!" she squeaks, but Teddy stops her.

"Shoo, you! There are no teeth for you now, and no visitors are allowed at night. You'll have to say goodbye."

Teddy is still cleaning up when the sneakiest one of all appears...

...THE TICKLE MONSTER!

"I'VE GOT HIM!" it squeals, but Teddy steps in before Noa can wake up.

"No tickling, no nibbling, no sock snatching or sniffing! NO visitors are allowed at night. You'll have to say goodbye!"

Oh noooooo...~

It's been a long night,
but Teddy feels proud.

Teddy can't wait for Noa
to wake up and play...

...but Teddy just needs
a tiny, tiny nap.

The sun is up, and Noa is full of energy and ready to have fun!

But TEDDY...!

Teddy has to get ready
for another busy night.